The Princess of Mantua

The Princess of Mantua

Marie Ferranti

Translated by Andrew Brown

ET REMOTISSIMA PROPE

Modern Voices

ïi institut français

This book is supported by the French Ministry for Foreign Affairs,
as part of the Burgess programme headed for the French Embassy
in London by the Institut Français du Royaume-Uni.
Ouvrage publié avec le concours du Ministère français chargé de la
culture – Centre National du Livre.

Published by Hesperus Press Limited
4 Rickett Street, London sw6 1ru
www.hesperuspress.com

The Princess of Mantua first published in French as *La Princesse
de Mantoue* in 2002
First published by Hesperus Press Limited, 2005
This edition published 2006
La Princesse de Mantoue © Editions Gallimard, 2002
This translation © Andrew Brown, 2005
Marie Ferranti asserts her moral right to be identified as the author
of this work under the Copyright, Designs and Patents Act 1988.

Designed and typeset by Fraser Muggeridge studio
Printed in Jordan by Jordan National Press

isbn: 1-84391-800-5
isbn13: 978-1-84391-800-4

To Lucien and Maria

I

Barbara of Brandenburg was ugly.

She was nearing fifty when Andrea Mantegna painted her, in 1470, at the side of her husband, Ludovico Gonzaga, surrounded by her numerous children and the court of Mantua.

'In the Camera Depicta,'[1] she wrote to her cousin, Maria of Hohenzollern, 'Mantegna has given me weary, jaundiced eyes, drawn up towards the temples like cats' eyes, and my face has no delicacy in it. Dare I admit that I am astonished at the way he has made me look? But Lady Julia, the dwarf, standing next to me, is staggeringly true to life, and so I too must resemble my portrait.

'The gaze of others is quite without indulgence for our defects and that of Mantegna is pitiless. I am grateful to him. Harshness, in the realm of the arts, is a virtue, and it is sometimes a good thing to see oneself as one is. My stupor, however, comes from the fact that people recognise me where I myself seem to see a stranger. This leads one to meditate more deeply on the matter. Are they dwelling on my superficial appearance rather than on what I really am? Who can say? You, perhaps, my dear Maria…'

Barbara did not bear a grudge against Mantegna for having painted her in this way. Never, as her voluminous correspondence attests, did she dream of having the fresco in the Camera

1. The Painted Chamber, in the Castello di San Giorgio, Mantua.

Depicta destroyed, as Isabella d'Este had a picture painted by Mantegna destroyed because the artist had neglected to make her look more beautiful – something the haughty Isabella had been unable to tolerate.

Barbara of Brandenburg's ambitions were aimed at something else.

Thus, she claimed that what she liked about Mantegna was the humility that made him write, in the dedication set over the door, that the Camera Depicta was a modest composition.

In the fifteenth century, Galeazzo Maria Sforza, Duke of Milan, said of 'this modest composition', with an admiration mingled with envy, that it was the most beautiful thing in the world.

In the seventeenth century, the Camera Depicta started to be called the 'Camera degli sposi'.[2] It has kept that name ever since. The princes of Mantua, Ludovico Gonzaga and Barbara of Brandenburg, were thus yoked together for all eternity.

* * *

It was towards the end of 1456 that Ludovico Gonzaga summoned Mantegna to Mantua; other artists – including highly respected figures such as Donatello – had declined his offer.

Mantegna seemed in no hurry to come and live in the home of his new master. The marquis, exasperated by Mantegna's delays, asked him to make his way to Mantua as soon as possible.

At the time, Mantegna was residing in Verona. He had just married the daughter of Jacopo Bellini, one of the most famous painters in Venice. He already enjoyed a certain celebrity and commissions were flooding in. He sent several missives to Ludovico Gonzaga. They are all in the same tenor. He assures

2. Generally known in English as the Bridal Chamber.

the marquis of his faithfulness, and deplores the fact that he cannot satisfy his request. 'Your Lordship,' he wrote, 'knows that my impatience to be in Mantua is every bit as great as is yours to see me there.'

However, the months went by and Mantegna still did not arrive.

Barbara played something of a part in getting him to come. However great a painter Mantegna might be, his procrastination irritated her. She complains of it several times in her letters.

Barbara made enquiries. She was not unaware of Mantegna's ambition and, to lure him to Mantua, convinced her husband to grant him a title of nobility.

Ludovico made a generous offer: he would bestow on the painter the escutcheon of his title embellished with the arms of the Gonzagas and a version of one of his own emblems. He added a remnant of red brocade damascened in silver from which Mantegna would be able to have a robe cut for wearing at court.

A month later, Mantegna was in Mantua. It had required nothing less than four years and a title of nobility to persuade him to come.

'The fish,' wrote Barbara to her cousin Maria of Hohenzollern, 'never resists the bait for long.'

In her letters, Barbara often demonstrates great good humour, a zest for life and an alert curiosity. After her husband's death, the tone changes; the language seems turned to stone. Especially in her replies to her younger daughter, Paola, Barbara sometimes evinces a hardness of heart that can turn into cruelty.

Her last letters remind one of the harshness of the profile depicted by Mantegna, and show what a good likeness the portrait he painted of Barbara of Brandenburg in the Bridal Chamber must have been. Appearances are never deceptive.

Barbara of Brandenburg was not yet ten years old when she arrived at the court of Mantua to marry Ludovico Gonzaga, first-born son of Francesco Gonzaga and Paola Malatesta.

She was a Hohenzollern on her mother's side, related to the emperor Sigismund. Springing from the flower of German nobility, her hand was promised, from earliest childhood, to the older son of the Gonzagas.

Barbara was warmly welcomed to the court of Mantua. This had nothing in common with the German court Barbara had just left. 'Compared to the Gonzagas, the Brandenburgs are country bumpkins,' wrote Barbara.

Surrounded by humanists, musicians and philosophers, Francesco Gonzaga wished to complete the girl's education. Although she could write and speak German, she struck him, according to Vittorino da Feltre, as 'shockingly ignorant'. Francesco Gonzaga had said of Barbara that her first name suited her down to the ground, which, coming from him, was of course not exactly a compliment.

Francesco and Paola Gonzaga did not draw any distinction between boys and girls. All their children – and it seems that Barbara was very soon considered as one of their own – enjoyed a very attentive upbringing. She was given Vittorino da Feltre as a tutor: he also taught Ludovico and his brothers – Carlo, Alessandro and Gianlucio.

He was a fine scholar and imparted to all the Gonzagas a taste for music, art and poetry. Until his death, in 1472, he was attached to the house of the Gonzagas. His correspondence is a valuable source of information on life at court in the fifteenth century. He played an absolutely essential role in the lives of Ludovico and Barbara.

Vittorino da Feltre taught Barbara Latin, Greek and the Lombard dialect, which Barbara always spoke and wrote, as she was happy to admit, with an unfailing pleasure. She used it just as much as her mother tongue, which she never abandoned, keeping up as she did a sustained correspondence with all her family and friends.

Vittorino also inculcated in Barbara of Brandenburg a love of poetry. She was well able, even in her sixties, to recite entire cantos of Dante, without omitting a single word.

Her daughter Barberina, in one of her letters, sings the praises of her prodigious memory, but also of the beauty and melodiousness of her voice.

However, the person who was most susceptible to poetry and understood it the best was Paola, her younger daughter, to whom Barbara was so cruel.

* * *

Three months after her arrival in Mantua, Barbara of Brandenburg married Ludovico Gonzaga. He was nineteen, she was barely ten. They were married in the Gonzaga chapel by the bishop of Mantua. Maria of Hohenzollern, not much older than Barbara, acted as the bride's witness.

The marriage was not consummated. The contract had stipulated that Ludovico Gonzaga would promise to wait until his wife reached puberty. Barbara hardly had time to see her husband before, shortly after the wedding, he fled from Mantua.

Of Ludovico, Barbara knew nothing, or almost nothing.

Ludovico Gonzaga was short and skinny, and he had inherited the fragile health of his mother, Paola Malatesta. By marrying into the Gonzagas, Paola brought with her an illness that was the lifelong despair of Barbara of Brandenburg: Paola Malatesta was a hunchback.

This ill health led his father to forbid Ludovico to go out riding for too long, and it led Ludovico to make but rare appearances in public. The worst rumours circulated in Mantua, not only at court, but also in town. The heir of the Gonzagas, it was said, would not be able to govern. There were not many people who held out much hope for the future of this ailing young man. Little by little, Ludovico retired to the sidelines. All eyes were now turned to Carlo, his younger brother.

Carlo was the prince of every heart.

How could anyone resist his charm? Vittorino is unstinting in his praise of this young man endowed with every grace. He could keep up philosophical and theological conversations with his master, read Greek and Latin at sight, was a peerless musician, and sang divinely.

Carlo was as robust as Ludovico was weakly, as outward-going as Ludovico was reserved. Ludovico knew that he could not compete with his brother.

Francesco Gonzaga found it difficult to conceal his preference for Carlo. Without an austere faith and a sense of justice sharpened by the physical pains inflicted on her by her illness, Paola might also have succumbed to the legitimate pride of having a son who was perfect in every way. She would always underplay Carlo's merits, not because she was unable to judge them at their true value, but because right was on the side of the first-born. The latter should not suffer any potentially damaging rivalry from within his own family. However, Paola too was afraid that Ludovico would never be the master of Mantua.

Vittorino da Feltre, in one of his letters, confides to his friend Gregorio Simeone, 'The whole court is convinced that the young Ludovico Gonzaga will not live long enough to govern; even his mother believes as much. Some people hope so. Personally, I wish for the right of seniority to be respected, despite the friendship that binds me to the younger brother, who, as you know, is closer to being the friend my heart desires than is Ludovico.'

Vittorino would keep his word when the time came.

In 1432, Francesco Gonzaga obtained from the emperor Sigismund, in exchange for a significant sum of money, the title of marquis for Ludovico. This title meant that he ranked just below a duke, the highest position in the imperial hierarchy.

This would transform Ludovico's life.

Hardly had he been married than he fled from Mantua in the middle of the night.

Barbara was informed a few hours later. The whole court was in uproar. Barbara presented herself as an 'obedient daughter' to Francesco and Paola, asking them what she ought to do. They asked her to stay in Mantua until Ludovico's return, and reassured her; the marriage had not been ruined; Ludovico could not remain absent for long.

The marquis Francesco and his wife initially refused to countenance the possibility that Ludovico had actually run away. They described it as a trip he had suddenly decided to take, but 'from the pallor of their faces,' says Vittorino da Feltre, 'everyone could judge of the gravity of the situation.'

Some time later, they were forced to yield to the evidence: Ludovico had presented himself to the Duke of Milan, Filippo Maria Visconti, and placed himself at his service.

What was the effect of this news on Barbara's inmost feelings?

She was still just a child. She was horrified. Her greatest fear was that she would have to leave the court of Mantua where she had found a real family: Francesco and Paola were always to be valuable allies to her. Nor did she want to leave the ladies of the court, some of whom were her own age and had become her playmates; and lastly, Barbara venerated her master Vittorino da Feltre, who saw in her 'a pupil whose curiosity and boldness of mind, in spite of her youth, greatly surpass her husband's'. This would not always be so, but Barbara displayed such qualities that she amazed the whole court.

Her sole consolation, if she was to return to Brandenburg, was that she would see Maria of Hohenzollern, her cousin, to whom she wrote every day; she opened her heart to her, hiding none of her thoughts or feelings. Nothing, except the periods of mourning that imposed silences lasting months on end, ever interrupted this correspondence. The two cousins rarely met in their youth, and later stopped seeing each other altogether, while continually promising to visit one another.

In 1479, Barbara even refused to go and see Maria, who was dying and asking for her. 'Since my own end cannot be long after yours,' she wrote to her, 'I wish to carry away with me the image of youth. When I think of you now, I imagine you as the young girl who came to attend my wedding. Do you remember? The happy days we then enjoyed! We spent our time babbling in our language, and chattered away from morning to night! Never again did we enjoy such freedom, granted with such grace by Paola Malatesta. She knew that our happiness was coming to an end, while we thought it was eternal.'

But at the time of Ludovico's flight, when Barbara privately told Maria of Hohenzollern of her distress, we do not know what Maria replied to her cousin, who was in despair and yet seemed to be putting such a brave face on things: most of her letters are lost.

For a few months, until Ludovico Gonzaga pledged his allegiance to Francesco Maria Sforza, Barbara held her peace. Later, that proved impossible. So she alerted her father Johann, nicknamed the Alchemist, because of the obsessive love of experiments that kept him locked away for whole nights in a wing of his castle.

Johann of Brandenburg was at a loss, and did not know what to do with this daughter whom he had known but little, and almost forgotten; he ordered her to wait.

Barbara of Brandenburg would wait for seven years. She would be grateful to Carlo for the kindness he showed her during the first period of Ludovico's absence. Carlo sought to distract her from her sorrow, played music to her and tried to teach her the harp, but Barbara was quite ungifted for music.

'I have no taste for music-making,' she said. 'In fact, I rather dislike it. I only enjoy listening to it and even then I do so with my eyes closed since I do not like to see the difficulties, however slight, that the musician has to overcome in order to produce sounds. I cannot listen to it for too long. I wonder how Carlo can play it for hours on end without getting tired. In my view, it makes you grow slack and flabby in character. I have been told that Ludovico does not like music as much as does his brother, which I am fully prepared to believe – otherwise he could not lead the life he does.'

و و و

During the first two years of Ludovico's absence, Barbara turned to religion. She prayed, had masses said, did penance to ensure that Ludovico would return. She had an especial devotion to St Sebastian. She spent her days and sometimes even her nights in the chapel of the Gonzagas. People grew alarmed and begged her to stop, but did not dare to command her. Indeed, there were fears for her reason. Their anxieties were misplaced. Barbara would never succumb to the raptures of mystic ecstasy: she mistrusted them. But what she would later, in her letters, call 'the discipline of conversation with God', in which she reflected on herself, would become a habit that she would never abandon. Even in the worst of circumstances, Barbara found time to reflect, to wait, as she prettily puts it, 'for my mind to cool down'. This wisdom was to be a valuable help for Ludovico, on more than one occasion.

Over the next five years, Barbara, whose sorrow had passed (after all, she admitted to Maria of Hohenzollern that she had even forgotten what her husband looked like), learnt the customs of the court, and made an intensive study of the arts of drawing and poetry, in particular Virgil and his *Aeneid*, of which she translated great swathes.

She loved the figure of Dido, and wrote to her cousin, 'Dido strikes me as my exact double. Just listen. "The Earth and Juno the guardian of marriage gave the first signal. Fires glittered in the heavens to celebrate their wedding, and on the mountain tops the Nymphs yelled the nuptial hymn. This was the first day of Dido's misfortunes, the first cause of her death."[3] However,' added Barbara, 'Dido was a victim of the Gods and I am merely the victim of my husband's folly.'

* * *

When he fled from Mantua, it was Ludovico Gonzaga's intention to become a soldier. He would be a warrior. He became an associate of that hothead, Niccolò Piccinino. He was nicknamed 'the Turk', on account of his ferocity.

When she heard this news, Barbara locked herself away for three days and prayed, taking neither food nor drink. Francesco Gonzaga cursed his son, and accused him of treason: Mantua

3. 'Prima et Tellus et pronuba Iuno / dant signum; fulsere ignes et conscius aether / conubiis, summoque ulularunt vertice Nymphae. / Ille dies primus leti primusque malorum / causa fuit.'

had always been the ally of Venice. His running away almost led to Ludovico's being disinherited. Paola opposed the move. She asked Francesco to pardon Ludovico. He refused.

Time was on Ludovico's side. Vittorino, his tutor, gave him his support. 'In my judgement,' he wrote, 'the value of a man who forges such a destiny for himself, against his very nature, is great and priceless.'

Ludovico Gonzaga built up such a reputation for himself throughout Italy that the pleadings of Vittorino da Feltre with Francesco bore fruit. Ludovico became an outstanding *condottiere*, at a time when Italy could point to men such as Colleoni and Francesco Maria Sforza, to whom he would be linked by an indissoluble friendship, even in the most difficult circumstances.

Eventually, Francesco Gonzaga pardoned him.

* * *

After such a long absence, the first meeting between Ludovico and Barbara is worth recounting.

Paola Malatesta had commissioned a portrait of Barbara and sent it to Ludovico, fearing – so says Vittorino – that the reunion of the young married couple might be spoiled if her son did not recognise Barbara: he had left behind a child and was now coming back to meet a young woman.

The whole court was summoned, the town festively decorated. The prodigal son was about to return.

'Ludovico is no longer the same, either psychologically or physically. His whole person radiates strength. His gaze, in especial, is unforgettable,' writes Vittorino.

Ludovico Gonzaga arrived at the head of an army of over four hundred men, all armed, with faces uncovered and unhelmed, in token of their peaceful intentions. Ludovico and his men had just reconquered Milan for Duke Francesco Maria Sforza – who had shown himself to be a generous man. Ludovico Gonzaga was now rich.

He never hesitated, thereafter, to sell his skill at warfare when the coffers of the Gonzagas needed replenishing. He would be seen on a battlefield, suffering an attack of gout, being carried on a litter to harangue his men and revive their ardour for the combat.

But, in this year 1440, Ludovico was a sturdy warrior, entering his town as victor. It was spring. The beauty of the men's armour, the clatter of the horses, the rattle of the weapons left the court and the inhabitants of Mantua dazzled by this soldier whose fame extended throughout northern Italy. They did not recognise, in this warrior filled with pride at his conquests, the sickly young man of bygone days. Ludovico was their prince.

At the gates of the town, Francesco was awaiting his son. Ludovico dismounted, and they embraced; then Ludovico went over and knelt piously at the feet of his mother, who lifted him up and gave him a kiss. All his brothers saluted him and placed one knee on the ground before him in sign of submission. Carlo too was there to participate in the triumph of Ludovico. Nothing, in his sumptuous courtly costume, apart from his tall stature and his straight back, distinguished him from his brothers. Did Ludovico and Carlo exchange a few words? Was their reunion marked by any special sign? We do not know. Nothing to suggest as much is noted in the account by Vittorino da Feltre, on which I am here drawing.

Ludovico's sisters were frozen in a respectful curtsy, but the first lady whom Ludovico raised from her bow was Barbara. He named her in a loud voice before all his men and the court, to show that he recognised her. He took her by the hand and led his wife over to Francesco Gonzaga in sign of submission to his paternal will. This gesture was acclaimed by loud hurrahs. The enormous procession set off. The feasts held in Ludovico's honour lasted three days and three nights.

'While I hardly remembered my marriage ceremony, my wedding night passed like a dream,' wrote Barbara. 'I was exhausted by the feasts celebrating your father's return – they had lasted two days. My mantle weighed down on my shoulders like a yoke. When I found myself in my chamber and they freed me of this burden, I immediately drowsed off. Ludovico slipped into my bed. I hardly had time to open my eyes. I felt a terrible weight bearing down on my chest. He rose from the bed, ordered me to get out, and checked that there was a bloodstain on the sheets. Whereupon he left to go hunting. I saw him only eight days later.'

This is what Barbara wrote in reply to her daughter Paola – many years later and with considerable coarseness – to convince her that there was nothing extraordinary in her German husband's behaviour, when Paola complained of his brusqueness towards her.

※ ※ ※

In 1444, Ludovico Gonzaga was in power.

He was the friend of humanists and artists. At the court of Mantua you could see Francesco Filelfo, Poggio Bracciolini, Donatello, Leon Battista Alberti or Luca Fancelli. Every day, Ludovico Gonzaga read Virgil, a poet dear to his heart, being a fellow Mantuan. He listened to music, for which all the Gonzagas had a real passion; but Ludovico had kept, from his military existence, a brusqueness of manner, a haughty tone, and a voice that he was continually raising.

'I shudder every time he says my name,' said Barbara.

Used as she was to the sophistication of the court of Mantua and the refinement of Carlo, whom she perhaps no longer regarded as 'a charming boy', since he was almost seventeen when Ludovico fled from Mantua, Barbara could not stand her husband's ways. She wrote to Maria of Hohenzollern that she would try to 'find some indirect way of touching him'.

This obscure expression reveals just what kind of person Barbara was. She would never oppose her husband or confront him directly. In order to convince him of anything, she whispered if he spoke loudly, suggested when he commanded, was all sweetness and light when he was brusque.

After all, Ludovico wrote to Francesco Maria Sforza, 'My wife speaks so softly that I always have to lean towards her to grasp the meaning of her words, so that everyone at court thinks we are forever caressing. We pass for the most closely knit couple in the world. As indeed we are.'

If Barbara had read these lines, she would have been in no doubt of the influence she had, and maybe she would have abused it. As she was unsure of it, she demonstrated a boundless patience and assumed an importance in Ludovico's eyes that only increased with time.

* * *

In 1445, Ludovico had reigned over Mantua for a year. His quickness of temper meant that no one dared express a single opinion unless it was flattering to him.

'Fear,' wrote Barbara to Maria of Hohenzollern, 'seals the most brazen mouths. Although a deafening hubbub drowns out everything at court, this deep silence rends my heart: it augurs no good.'

Used as he was to vanquishing and commanding, Ludovico Gonzaga had forgotten the lessons of his master, Vittorino da Feltre: he no longer listened to anyone. Barbara could foresee the dangers of such an attitude. Carlo Gonzaga now kept his distance from court but had not given up Mantua. Several men, even at court, were his supporters. Ludovico knew this and did not hesitate to show contempt for them, mocking them openly, which aggravated their rancour.

The thing that most surprises anyone who examines his life – Ludovico is recognised as one of the most enlightened aristocrats of his time – is that he now reigned over Mantua as a despot.

'I do not know what has become of my teaching,' writes Vittorino. 'We must be patient. Ludovico is sharpening his weapons, which are still blunt. I am waiting for him to weary of this, but no one with an observant mind can fail to notice that, if he delays, his delay may prove fatal to him.'

When Ludovico Gonzaga later reached his full measure, Vittorino attributed it to the experience of power. 'The heart hardens to bronze,' he wrote. Not for a single moment did he imagine that Barbara lay behind these changes.

Barbara was no politician, but, at the start of her marriage, she claimed she was curious to know what was said by wagging tongues.

To do this, she would use a stratagem that would bolster Ludovico's power and, in addition, give him great delight. Her husband's character would be definitively changed. In just a few months, Barbara would turn Ludovico the warrior into a man of wisdom. She would make of 'the Turk' the most long-suffering of Christians.

On Ludovico's return, Barbara of Brandenburg was still a girl, full of imagination. She was seventeen. Experience of the world had not yet deprived her of her carefree character, and the trial she had endured had not spoiled her natural gaiety. She had a passion for theatre, games and the dances, of which she never tired – difficult though this is to imagine given her corpulence. From her youngest years, she complained of her girth, which 'hindered her even in her slightest movements'.

Barbara had inherited from her father a liking for extraordinary things, and a taste for improvisation and freedom, but she was also able to *rein herself in*.

This alliance of reason and imagination, tempered by the education she received from Vittorino da Feltre, performed miracles. The court of Mantua was one of the gayest in Europe, at a time when gaiety in society was a duty like that of waging war on one's enemies. Barbarity and the most exquisite politeness went hand in hand among those great Renaissance lords.

In any case, Venice was not so far away, and while Ludovico Gonzaga was never its ally, the court of Mantua did not neglect to draw inspiration from Venetian sophistication and its changing fashions. The arrival of Mantegna in Mantua merely accentuated this influence – which was also *indirect*.

* * *

In her youth, Barbara liked nothing so much as to go out walking in the streets of Mantua, doing the rounds of the markets and the stalls. She was forbidden to do so unless she was accompanied by an army of domestics and servant girls, not to mention armed men. Thus it was that Barbara, with a servant at her side, and unknown to her husband, would go round Mantua dressed as a peasant woman. 'I want,' she wrote, 'to find out what the common people really think – their opinion is by no means the most foolish.'

Barbara watched, listened, concealed her identity, and passed herself off under the name of Maria, something which gave her great delight.

'I have the feeling,' she wrote to her cousin, 'that I am sharing my enjoyment of these games with you. You are keeping me company.'

Maria claimed to be 'stupefied, but delighted'. Barbara continually surprised her. In the few letters from Maria of Hohenzollern that have come down to us, Maria says she is always expecting her cousin to relate something extraordinary to her; she eggs her on, encourages her, wants her to 'dispel her boredom', and Barbara obliges.

* * *

Barbara's subterfuge did not remain secret for long. When Ludovico learnt that his wife was going out without an escort, he was furious, but Barbara persuaded him to find out for himself what the townsfolk of Mantua, rather than the court, were thinking. The people were discontented; taxes were too heavy, and the men who were – wrongly – called 'the Milanese', and who constituted Ludovico's close guard, were barely tolerated.

Barbara related to Maria a scene that occurred in a tavern. This letter was unknown to the general public for a long time. It was revealed only in the 1930s, thanks to the dispersal of the collection belonging to the celebrated Marquis of Ventivoglio that the City of Mantua bought up. It is now in the print room of the city museum, where it is conserved in light-controlled surroundings: and it is here that I was able to consult it, thanks to Pietro Mazetti, the curator.

Despite its length, I cannot resist the pleasure of quoting it in its entirety.[4]

We had to wait until the court had gone to bed. It was after ten in the evening. Ludovico and I found it very difficult to conceal our impatience. We hardly touched our suppers. This excursion had been prepared long in advance, and we would not have missed it for anything in the world. They ask why we were in such a bad mood. We showed even greater ill humour. Seeing that our temper was merely getting worse and worse, they asked for permission to withdraw and took their departure earlier than usual, to our great relief. Only Francesco Rialoto, the captain of Ludovico's guards, Teresa, my *cameriera*, whom I had known, as you will remember, from the time I arrived in Mantua, Ludovico and I were in on the secret. Imagine, my dear Maria, a deserted Mantua, and us leaving the castle on foot, without escort, poorly dressed, champing at the bit, running, panting and laughing at the fine trick we were playing.

After following narrow little alleys that twisted and turned so much it made you dizzy, we finally arrived outside the tavern to which Francesco was taking us.

We paused for a while to get our breath back and examine our faces. I arranged my headgear, and reminded Teresa to address me familiarly; Ludovico did likewise with Francesco,

4. Translated from the German by Pietro Mazetti in *Lettere di Barbara di Brandeburgo* (Einaudi). Translated from the Italian by Marie Ferranti.

his captain, and, with beating hearts, we plunged into the noisy, smoky room, with its stench and filth.

This tavern is open all night long to all the empty-headed dreamers of Mantua, the mercenaries with their shoddy equipment and shabby clothes, and women young and old, some of them with their children sleeping on the tables or at their feet, right there on their floor. The air was so foul that it made my eyes and throat sting. We had to get used to the stench and the acrid odour of soot.

Ludovico pushed his way through to find a place for us at the far end of a table already laden with victuals and wine. I made as if to sit down and Teresa was just about to curtsy, before I signalled to her with my eyes and she stopped. Fortunately, nobody had noticed. I swore. Teresa blushed crimson and Ludovico pulled such a face that I cannot remember it without laughing, so great was his amazement at hearing me swear. Actually, do you know how I picked up those swear words? In the summer, such oaths would waft into my room through the open window. In the courtyard, the grooms held forth freely. I noted that these words sometimes came to me quite naturally. Well, believe you me, they appease wrath more efficiently than those we usually employ. Anyway, back to our tavern. Francesco was the one most at his ease. He knew people there, and greeted some of the soldiers who wanted to join us, but Ludovico made a sign to Francesco, who shooed them away.

At our table, everyone rubbed shoulders: young and old, men and women. After a quarter of an hour, we had overcome our initial amazement. There were three strapping great lads sitting opposite me, and two very young girls who were extremely merry and, I think, a bit drunk.

Food and drink were brought to us: mutton stew and soup, accompanied by a not very nice wine. We ate and drank with great pleasure, since we had come a long way and worked up an appetite.

To strike up conversation with our neighbours at table, we offered them some wine. Teresa, who had grown tipsy with the wine and whom I had never seen making so bold, exaggerated her Lombard accent and called out to one of the two women facing her. The young woman, who struck me as rather forward – and as you will see, I was not wrong – introduced herself: her name was Luisa, she had arrived in Mantua only shortly before, and came from the country.

We introduced ourselves in turn. Conversation was soon flowing, and grew increasingly heated. At first, neither Ludovico nor I took part. I confess that I even had some difficulty in following it. Ludovico, seeing my perplexity, translated what I did not understand, and then my ear became attuned to those sounds, more raucous and less delicate than those we were used to hearing. I ventured to utter a few words, grew emboldened and, in allusive but perfectly comprehensible terms, went so far as to speak ill of Ludovico. Imagine his astonishment. He almost choked. A big lad, with a big mouth, intervened.

'Allow me to introduce myself: Andrea, of Verona, at your service. Ludovico may have conquered Milan, but he hasn't conquered me!' – whereupon he swigged back a great mouthful of wine.

Ludovico could not restrain himself, in spite of the kick I gave him under the table.

'And what has our prince done to deserve your anger?' he said.

He: 'What? It's been six months since I was dismissed. His father had me in his employment, but as for him – zilch!'

Ludovico: 'What did you do for my' – another kick – 'er... for Marquis Francesco?'

He: 'I looked after the horses. I was fed and lodged, but now that his son's brought back all those men, there's no jobs for *us* any more; they're all taken by the Milanese. For Marco' – the man sitting next to him – 'same thing. What do you expect him to do except get drunk?'

Marco: 'Hold on, pal! Speak for yourself; you're as drunk as a lord from morning to night...'

Ludovico: 'That will do! What was *your* job?'

Marco: 'Gardener. I went to have a look at the castle gardens the other day; they're not what they were when I was working there. With the Milanese, they've gone to ruin. And as for the streets, I'd rather not talk about them. They stink. In the evenings, you've every chance of getting your throat slit. The Milanese get handsomely paid, but when it comes to doing the rounds, they're never there!'

Andrea: 'Marco's right. The thing is, we're out every night. There's only thieves who are awake, that's the thing, and the soldiers are all asleep!'

We sat open-mouthed and let the conversation take its course, nodding our agreement from time to time, but no longer talking. The wine had inflamed people's minds. Things were starting to turn dangerous. The women drank as much as the men. Ludovico tried to look cheerful, but he did not succeed. He looked sombre. Seeing how unhappy he looked, Luisa came over to him and started to flirt. I shot a black look at her, but in vain – that one was used to ignoring her rivals. Ludovico, as I could see, was greatly amused at my resentment.

'You're really caught in the snare!' he said to me when Luisa finally let him draw breath.

'Not as much as you, it seems,' I retorted.

'Too true!' said Ludovico with a laugh, since Luisa had restored his good humour to him.

'We ought to think about getting back,' said Francesco.

The evening was drawing to a close. Teresa had gone to sleep. We had to shake her before she would wake up. But no sooner had the others seen that we were leaving than they gathered round us. They insisted on accompanying us home, for safety's sake. We were obliged to sit down and have another drink. I was so tired I could hardly keep my eyes open. We had every difficulty imaginable in persuading our companions to allow us to leave. Night was almost over by the time we were finally able to rise from table and take our leave. We had to put up with their hugs and promise to see them again.

We returned via the garden gate. Ludovico never left my side. When we awoke, it was broad daylight. That, my dear Maria, is how we spend our time. I will tell you what effect our labours had the next time I write. Yours,

– Barbara of Brandenburg

What did Ludovico learn from all this? Probably not much from what the two drunkards had said, in those words reported in such lively style by Barbara – but a political lesson, certainly. Barbara realised as much; she wrote, 'What made the greatest impression on Ludovico was the freedom of speech of those lowly folk, compared to the grimaces of the lords and ladies at court. He saw this as a sign he must change. So change he did.'

Indeed, Ludovico Gonzaga remedied everything. He had the town paved, and constructed new buildings on the market, and the arcades of the Palace of Reason, and a new bridge between the Pusterla and Cerese gates; and he ordered Leon Battista Alberti, the greatest architect of his age, to build the churches of Sant'Andrea and San Sebastiano, the latter so dear to Barbara's heart, and finally the famous tower whose clock was perfected by the mathematician Bartolomeo Manfredi. 'It is marvelled at by all,' wrote Vittorino da Feltre. 'People come from all over the world to admire it.'

In 1460, the world, for the Mantuans, had narrow limits; it extended no further than a few neighbouring Christian courts; America did not yet exist. In any case, even if he had known of its existence, the chances are that Vittorino would not have spoken any differently.

Over a century later, Mantua was renowned for being, in the words of Montaigne, who visited it in 1580, 'one of the cleanest and best policed towns in Italy'. As he made his way through it, in a hurry to get to Venice, Montaigne did not stop to visit the Palazzo del Tè, erected on the site of an old stable by Federico Gonzaga, Marquis of Mantua and the son of Isabella d'Este, of whom we have a portrait painted by Titian.

The Gonzagas who succeeded Ludovico followed his example in their mode of governing. They had exquisite, sometimes strange tastes. They were never put off by eccentricities. Thus Vasari can say of the Palazzo del Tè that it was one of the most extraordinary things of that time, which was not short of extraordinary things.

The Gonzagas still have the ability to amaze.

Following Barbara's advice, Ludovico, in the first year of his reign, did not wage war on Carlo Gonzaga. 'He does not want to owe Mantua to the blood of his brother,' Barbara wrote to Maria of Hohenzollern. 'It would have been easy to do so. He has an army ready to obey him, hardened by the reconquest of Milan. His triumph is assured, but Ludovico does not want to embark on a war that he knows is already won in advance; his power is still fragile, he needs to preserve it.'

On his brother's return, Carlo Gonzaga's hopes of ruling faded. He quarrelled with Vittorino da Feltre, who supported Ludovico.

'With Ludovico,' wrote Vittorino, 'I support law, order and justice.'

Carlo Gonzaga would be reconciled with his old master shortly before his death. But in 1444 he left the court and withdrew to his own lands to prepare his revenge. He had not lost all hope of being the master of Mantua.

What did Ludovico do, since he would not wage war? Ludovico bought up everything at a premium price: Carlo's lands, domains and castles. He paid a fortune for what he could have got for nothing. Carlo yielded. He retired to a castle, some distance from Mantua, so as to present no threat to Ludovico.

Carlo was gradually overwhelmed by melancholy. All idea of conquest abandoned him. He gave sumptuous feasts, invited the greatest artists of his time, summoned musicians. Of all this activity, no trace was to remain.

Carlo stayed in his palace, eaten up with sorrow.

'He can be seen walking through the icy dawn,' says Vittorino, 'like a great, solitary shade.'

Carlo Gonzaga had lost all his self-confidence; he swelled to an enormous size, and lost his teeth. He had only just turned thirty-four, but he looked like an old man. Carlo's wife wrote to Ludovico to warn him of the peril his brother was in. 'Let my brother go to meet his destiny,' replied Ludovico.

Nonetheless, he granted Vittorino da Feltre permission to go and visit him. Barbara accompanied him. Of her brother-in-law, whom she had known as 'the most likeable boy in the world', she said that he had become hideously ugly. 'I have nothing to complain of,' she wrote to Ludovico. 'Carlo does everything to make my stay pleasant, but the mere sight of him completely spoils it for me. I am longing to return.'

As for Vittorino, he was deeply upset. 'I had looked forward to seeing him again with such joy,' he writes. 'There is nothing left of the Carlo Gonzaga I knew hardly ten years ago.'

Carlo died in 1456, at the age of thirty-nine. Ludovico had never seen him again. He paid every honour to his brother, decreed three days' mourning, and had him buried in the chapel of the Gonzagas. Carlo's story was at an end.

Barbara, who perhaps remembered the sorrows she herself had endured in her childhood, and feared for her nephew and niece the example of the depravity their father had set them, asked Ludovico to take Carlo's children into his care. They would receive the best possible upbringing.

'Gentilia's resemblance to her father,' wrote Barbara, 'made me fear that Ludovico would hate her, but Gentilia has him spellbound. No sooner does she appear than Ludovico forgets everyone else. With Gentilia, something of the presence of Carlo is restored to us at court. His son Evangelista is also much loved by us and returns the affection we bear him. As far as his children are concerned, Carlo seems never to have existed. It is true that he neglected them and left them fallow, as our excellent Vittorino put it, simply getting them to play and listen to music, and to declaim poetry, for which they have kept a taste – a taste that is more reliable than that of almost anyone else at court.'

Ludovico was fond of Evangelista, but preferred Gentilia, who loved him tenderly. Barbara would suffer from the passion that Ludovico felt for this girl.

They say she can be recognised on the fresco in the Bridal Chamber, her head gracefully inclined. In all the movements of her body, captured by Mantegna, there is that suppleness of which illness had deprived most of Barbara's children – but there is also sadness in her eyes and a melancholy that makes Gentilia's beauty fragile and precious.

Ludovico loved her enough not to send her far away to be married. He wanted Gentilia to be present at every festivity. She was the only woman with whom he discussed poetry and music in private, and whose advice he sometimes asked in public, not on political and military matters, but on the arts. After all, Vittorino da Feltre wrote, 'Gentilia has inherited her father's perfect good taste.'

Barbara's firmly maintained principles were: calm and moderation. She never complained. Still, in her correspondence we find this remark: 'Ludovico balks at marrying off Gentilia. No suitor is good enough for her. I am urging him to do so for fear she may never find one. Today, we came to an agreement on the matter. But he made this one condition: Gentilia will wed a Lombard gentleman. He cannot stand the idea of being separated from her. I acquiesced in everything. It strikes me as pointless to try and extinguish a passion that will die away of its own accord if it is not fuelled by obstacles.'

What admirable lucidity Barbara showed! She knew that the bonds that united her to Ludovico were of another order: her children, and the government of Mantua.

2

'It is easy to imagine,' writes Vittorino da Feltre, 'Ludovico's joy at the news of the birth of his first son, Federico. The mourning period for Francesco Gonzaga was finally over. Mantua could breathe again. The town was decked with flags. Cannon shots were fired, and three days were spent eating, drinking and dancing, while the whole court filed past the bed of the young woman who had just given birth.'

Vittorino da Feltre does not say a word about the absence of Carlo, who was not invited to the celebrations, any more than was Alessandro, another of Ludovico's brothers, who was suffering from melancholy, shut away in a castle far away from Mantua. The death of his father Francesco, a year earlier, had definitively deprived him of his wits.

Vittorino also says nothing about Paola Malatesta. Since her husband's death, she still lived at court, but rarely made an appearance.

We know from Barbara's letters to Maria of Hohenzollern that Paola Malatesta came to visit Barbara only on the day after she had given birth.

On the day Federico was born, Paola Malatesta was so ill that she sent a note to Barbara, accompanied by a magnificent present; she absolutely wanted Barbara to have it now, without further delay.

It was a luxurious trousseau, in gold and silver embroidery, presented in two painted *cassoni*,[5] decorated with biblical scenes: the sacrifice of Abraham and the judgement of Solomon.

The beauty of the trousseau aroused the admiration of the whole court. However, Barbara confessed that she could not stand the sight of these two chests. 'Those images are familiar to me, but I cannot bear seeing them nor can I have them taken away from my room without causing grave offence to my mother-in-law and my husband. I have had them put away near my bed, so that my gaze will not fall on them accidentally. It seems to me as if I were seeing my son's future in those suspended atrocities. Perhaps it is the novelty of my state that is filling me with such dreadful ideas?'

Would Barbara remember the terrible feelings that had spoiled her joy as a new mother when she later commissioned some sumptuous *cassoni* from Mantegna for the wedding of her youngest daughter, Paola? I doubt it: if so, her gift was all the crueller.

But the most difficult thing Barbara had to endure was her mother-in-law's visit. 'When I saw Paola Malatesta,' she said, 'I felt the blood freezing in my veins.'

He made her appearance hanging on Ludovico's arm.

'In full mourning, bent double, her hands clutching her son's arm, she walked with extraordinary slowness; her hump covered half of her back, her head was bowed towards the ground, she strained her neck to try and look up, and thereupon showed a face marked by continual suffering and sorrow.

'The newborn child was presented to Paola Malatesta, but she could not take him, since she can barely move, having no strength, and her fingers are all twisted. Paola Malatesta,' wrote Barbara, 'sensed all the horror that the sight of her aroused. She took her leave as soon as she was able.'

5. Chests.

Since the death of Francesco, Paola's state had considerably worsened. She could hardly stand. On the day of her visit, Barbara discovered the extent of the ravages of her illness. 'Paola,' she says, 'had always received me lying in bed, her head propped up by cushions, dressed in white, smothered in lace to hide her defects, and appearing to me no more ugly than any woman of her age. In my chamber, she looked like a fearsome animal – like a monster, to tell you the truth.'

After that, Paola refused to show herself in public. She renounced the world. 'Every day,' wrote Barbara, 'Ludovico goes to her apartments, enquiring after her health and the progress of her malady, and filled with pity for her.'

Even though she was grateful to Paola Malatesta for having always supported her in the past, seeing her, on the day after her son's birth, caused Barbara the most grievous torments. For months afterwards, Barbara said she could not summon up any of the zest she had once shown for the games that had delighted her in her youth. She wrote to her cousin, 'I am no longer as cheerful, and I have lost my taste for telling stories.'

Between 1441 and 1460, Barbara of Brandenburg had ten children. After Federico came Francesco, Gianfrancesco, Cecilia, Susanna, Dorotea, Rodolfo, Barberina, Paola and Ludovico.

These twenty years represented the apogee of the reign of Ludovico and Barbara, but they also included some of the cruellest years of their lives.

Barbara was obsessed by the idea that her children would be hunchbacks. The numerous letters to Maria of Hohenzollern, and to her friends and relations, show that not a day went by without Barbara keeping a close eye on her children, recognising, surmising or fearing the appearance of Paola Malatesta's illness.

'While the nursemaids or chambermaids are dressing them, I hide behind the wall-hangings: they have been ordered to present the children to me in profile, and I look at their backs. Admittedly, Cecilia is so tiny and her limbs so frail that this is pointless. Dorotea is chubby-cheeked and plump. Rodolfo is ruddy and choleric. I do not think he will be a hunchback, but his skittish character causes me more anxiety than I can say. Only Francesco is, so far, a child after my own heart. He does not enjoy good health but he is sweet-natured and firm of temperament. Federico has taken on Alessandro's melancholy.'

Gentilia Gonzaga was brought up with the daughters of Ludovico and Barbara. Vittorino da Feltre, now an old man, was appointed as their tutor, and Filelfo taught the boys. 'Apart from Dorotea and Susanna,' writes Vittorino, 'the daughters of Ludovico Gonzaga are all hunchbacked. The worst affected is the youngest, Paola; given that name in memory of her grandmother, she seems to have inherited not only her hump but also her sharp mind.

'Ludovico has eyes only for Gentilia, the daughter of his late brother Carlo. She is the model of grace, and eclipses by her beauty and her wit all of Ludovico's daughters. They are not jealous of her, something which never fails to astonish me. They are all exquisitely kind to their cousin. In this family, things that elsewhere would be considered extraordinary are seen as quite commonplace.

'As for Barbara, I have always prized her wit and the boldness of her character, but, now I am older, I appreciate ever more the simplicity with which she talks of the terrible fate of certain of her children. I see this as an elevated and unique form of compassion.'

Barbara's wisdom doubtless commanded that she hide feelings whose meanness repelled her and whose effects might later give her cause for regret. The marquise was subtle enough to size up those effects, and lucid enough to realise that it would be a mistake to ignore their potentially dangerous consequences.

In 1448, Ludovico Gonzaga decided to move the court to the Castello di San Giorgio. Ludovico was now a very popular prince, and we do not know by what peril he felt threatened enough to leave the princely residence erected by his father and decorated by Pisanello and settle in San Giorgio, which was an obscure fortress adjoining his palace.

He immediately called on Mantegna to decorate his new residence. In fifteenth-century Italy, it was usual for princes to possess a ceremonial painted room, the *camera*, a big reception hall, the *sala*, and a chapel where mass was celebrated every day.

In the ceremonial room, all the wealth was exhibited on the walls, where sumptuous hangings and tapestries in dazzling colours hanging from rails ran round over the walls and doors. These drapes were also to be found in the Bridal Chamber, but here they were painted: the Bridal Chamber is the chamber of illusions.

* * *

In 1457, Ludovico's position had never been so strong. He was recognised as one of the foremost *condottieri* in Italy. There was no longer any opposition to him. Carlo had just died and, in any case, the only danger he now constituted was to himself. Nobody in Lombardy would have dared attack the ally of the powerful Francesco Sforza, duke of Milan.

And yet, this was the year that Federico, the elder son of the house of the Gonzagas, chose to leave the court – not to wage war, as his father had done before him, which would have been a glorious enterprise, but to follow a lower-class woman with whom he had suddenly fallen in love.

Whether it was due to the shadow cast by the mourning for Francesco, the absence of Carlo and Alessandro, or the tardy arrival of his grandmother, Paóla Malatesta, on the day after his birth (which Barbara always considered as a sign of ill omen), Federico Gonzaga was a glum child and would remain so.

'Your Federico is melancholy by nature, and Aristotle teaches us that the melancholy are ingenious,' wrote Filelfo, the great humanist, to Ludovico Gonzaga. He exhorted him to provide for his son's literary education.

While Federico loved the arts – how could he not have been susceptible to them, in such a family? – he was also attracted to war and commerce; above all else, he loved architecture. But he did nothing with his life. Gian Pietro Galloni, an old courtier, would say of him, 'He is hunchbacked, gallant and courteous.' It was not much.

We know nothing of the woman he loved, but Federico was driven by his love to go all the way to Naples where his lover abandoned him.

After some time, he fell into the greatest poverty. Barbara sent emissaries, who found him in one of the poorest districts of Naples, 'filthy, flea-ridden and ill'.

In the greatest alarm, Barbara implored Ludovico to take pity. Ludovico forgave his son and gave his wife permission to go to Naples.

She wrote to Ludovico, 'Federico is more or less recovered, but he is still very thin. His eyes are clouded and he seems so disturbed that for a moment I feared he had lost his wits. He would not have been the first in your family or mine to have met with this misfortune.'

Barbara of Brandenburg did not stay long in Naples, which she said she did not like. The sight of the sea was highly disagreeable to her. In this month of June 1457, she felt oppressed by the heat. None of the region's beauty moved her. Her only thought was to return home, which she did at the earliest opportunity. She was pregnant with Barberina.

No sooner had he returned to Mantua than Federico was married off to Margarete of Wittelsbach and provided no more occasion for gossip.

'Federico,' said his mother, during his reign in Mantua, 'is irregular in all he does. He wearies of everything just as quickly as he had developed a craze for it.'

His reign, which was short – begun in 1475, it ended in 1484 – was one of the most lacklustre in the entire Gonzaga period, which lasted for three hundred years.

But let us return to the first years of the reign of Ludovico Gonzaga.

Since 1450, Ludovico Gonzaga had reinforced his ties with Francesco Maria Sforza, who made of Milan one of the most prosperous domains in Italy. When there was talk of marrying off Susanna to the first-born of the Sforzas, in 1463, this union seemed both legitimate and astute. However, Susanna, who until then had shown no sign of the illness, developed a hump. Ludovico Gonzaga broke off the engagement and, after a new agreement had been drawn up, Susanna was replaced by Dorotea: 'beautiful and straight-backed,' as he himself wrote to the Duke of Milan.

'The only woman who can be compared to Gentilia is Dorotea. If God spares her, she will surpass them all,' Barbara had written to her cousin.

God did not spare her.

And yet the auspices seemed perfectly favourable: the two young people liked one another. Galeazzo Sforza had been in love with Dorotea from childhood on. As soon as the engagement was proclaimed, not a week went by without him sending her sumptuous presents, nor a week without him coming to visit her. The court of Mantua was in a state of permanent festivity.

It lasted a year. Suddenly, this assiduous courtship came to an end; the visits became less frequent, and the presents fewer. 'Dorotea's lover is neglecting her,' noted Barbara, in alarm.

An emissary from Francesco Sforza shed light on this 'neglect': the Duke of Milan was afraid that Dorotea might fall ill like her sister Susanna, even though nothing indicated this would happen. He decided to seek medical opinion. He took on the responsibility of sending doctors from Milan.

Ludovico and Barbara Gonzaga understood this anxiety and bowed to all the Sforzas' demands, but several of Barbara's letters show the distress she was in during this whole period.

'When I saw those three men dressed in long black robes laying hands on my daughter,' she wrote, 'I thought I was going to faint. They stayed shut away, with Don Pietro' – the priest – 'for two long hours, and departed as they had come, leaving us in ignorance.'

'If the calm and strength of Ludovico were any less, I do not know what would become of me. I feel as if my body and mind had been separated. I hear myself talking as if it were some other woman speaking through my mouth. I do not dare utter anything but commonplace remarks for fear of losing myself in the labyrinth of my thoughts, I laugh with the others even though I do not know why, I eat, I sleep, I dress, all of this in the greatest indifference of spirit, as my mind is always preoccupied by my poor child, delivered into the hands of those three black devils.'

Dorotea endured all these trials – the doctors would return three times to Mantua – but, says Barbara, 'what is tearing her apart is Galeazzo's silence. I cannot stop thinking, even though I am obliged to keep my thoughts to myself, that the fiancé will wriggle out of his oath even if it means committing treason. Dorotea is but a shadow of her former self. Ludovico says he has caused her ruin. The other day, he wept as he confided to me, "God is punishing me for my pride." – "Is it God, or Francesco Sforza?" I replied.'

'It has been announced that Galeazzo Sforza is to wed the sister-in-law of the King of France.'

Finally, a single line, almost illegible as the writing is so shaky: 'Dorotea is dying.'

* * *

For several months, the correspondence between Barbara of Brandenburg and Maria of Hohenzollern was interrupted.

Francesco's elevation to the rank of cardinal came just in time to give new hope to a devastated family. Francesco Sforza used all his power to ensure that this appointment was ratified. He could not manage without his alliance to Ludovico Gonzaga, and maybe he felt some regret that things should have ended this way. After all, Ludovico had written to him that Dorotea had died of sorrow (*castigo*) and the pains she had endured (*dolori sopportati*).

'She is an angel,' replied Francesco Sforza, 'and she has returned to paradise.'

Almost a year after Dorotea's death, something happened which nobody at the court of Mantua believed would ever happen. The

Gonzagas emerged from the dull pain into which the death of their daughter had plunged them.

It was Barbara, as we know from her writings, who asked Mantegna to depict the moment at which the elevation of her second son Francesco to the rank of cardinal was announced.

While the painting of Mantegna's fresco was a consolation for the misfortune that had just overwhelmed the entire Gonzaga family, the composing of the Camera Depicta would provide a necessary distraction from obsessive and prolonged brooding over Dorotea's death.

It occupied the minds of everyone at court for months, so that oblivion little by little engulfed even Dorotea's name, which no one now dared pronounce in front of Barbara and Ludovico, for fear of rekindling a pain that, in fact, had finally faded away.

The memory of her sister Susanna, who had taken holy orders, and also died in the flower of her age, was piously preserved. Her name often came up in conversation.

Dorotea was never mentioned again. The name of the woman who had been passionately loved was now uttered only on the day when mass was said for the dead.

3

In 1464, the chapel of San Giorgio was finished, and Mantegna could start on the composition of the Camera Depicta, with which, as I have said, Barbara was to be greatly involved. The scenes were not, as one might think, painted from life, but composed and indeed corrected on the orders of Ludovico or Barbara.

Something that might seem counter to our conception of art – the fact that the person commissioning it could intervene in a work's execution and even its conception – was commonplace in the fifteenth century. The painter himself asked for, indeed expected, guidance. Mantegna was constantly anxious to satisfy the Gonzagas. He merely complained that he was never paid on time. Ludovico retorted that his slowness to pay was a response to the artist's slowness to paint. 'Why criticise me for what you have always inflicted on *me*: this waiting that sometimes makes me worry myself sick, as rust devours iron?' he wrote to Mantegna, who was claiming his due.

'The slowness of the artist comes from the demands of his art and that of Ludovico comes merely from contempt (*disprezzo*) for his art,' replied Mantegna.

These were simply rhetorical skirmishes. Mantegna was to remain attached to the house of the Gonzagas for almost fifty years. He loved Mantua so much, Vasari tells us, that he had a marvellous house built there for himself, which could rival the houses of great lords in beauty.

If Ludovico Gonzaga had not demonstrated a very elevated awareness of his role and his rank, Mantegna could not have executed the Camera Depicta of the Palazzo di San Giorgio.

This 'slowness' often took the form of an interruption of several months. Mantegna took over ten years to finish the Camera Depicta. But, from Barbara of Brandenburg, Ludovico Gonzaga had learnt the art of patience.

When Mantegna was shown the chamber destined for ceremonial use, he was aghast at the room's dimensions, the badly positioned openings, and the lack of light that came through them.

'I intimated to her Ladyship, Barbara Gonzaga, that the ceremonial chamber is not well suited.

' "Well," she retorted, "help us to forget the fact!" '

'This casual attitude, which you always find in people quite ignorant of our art' – wrote Mantegna to Jacopo Bellini, his father-in-law – 'makes my blood boil. How can you put wall-hangings on twisted walls?'

'Paint them!' replied Jacopo.

Mantegna was not convinced. He waited for several weeks before doing anything. He did not know where to start. He shut himself away in the room for several hours a day, with portfolios and quills of every sort that he cut himself; he had the windows walled in and the room lit *a giorno* by dozens of candles to show up the imperfections of the wall, which he minutely examined and noted.

When Ludovico asked him for the results of his labours, he presented him with a plan of the room, showing the places where the frescoes would be. Those places were empty. The paintings were shown by blanks. Ludovico could not conceal his disappointment and anger. 'Several months – for *that*? So don't you have any idea of what you are going to do?' he asked.

'Not of what I'm going to do, no,' replied Mantegna. 'But I do know where I am going to put it.'

Mantegna knew the subject that would figure on the frescoes – it had been imposed on him. On one wall, he would depict the announcement at the court of Mantua of the elevation of Francesco, the son of Ludovico and Barbara Gonzaga, to the rank of cardinal; on the other wall, his arrival and the meeting with his father and his brothers, who had come to greet him at the city gates.

Mantegna wrote to Jacopo, 'How can I, not explain to his Lordship – he is perfectly capable of understanding it – but make him admit that the preparation of the wall is more important than the painting itself and that there is absolutely no point painting on a wall that can't *hold* the colour?'

Barbara avoided him. 'I know how very talented Mantegna is,' she wrote to Maria of Hohenzollern, 'but seeing him squandering his time like this irritates me in the highest degree. Note that this anger greatly preoccupies me and distracts me from my sorrows. Even just a year ago, I would not have bothered in the slightest to find out how his work was advancing. I am eager for him to start, since an artist's talent has always helped a cardinal rise to the rank of pope. And then all my wishes would be fulfilled, and my sorrows, without being wiped away, would be lessened by that immense joy, and I think that we can now await the outcome with all reasonable hope.'

If the depiction of this scene – the announcement of Francesco's elevation to the rank of cardinal – was essential for the Gonzagas, it was not so for Mantegna. 'I have to give body,' he said, 'to this room that does not have one.'

Preparing the wall required several months. Mantegna demanded 'the purest spring water' to wash the wall before laying the *trusilar* – the layer of plaster that was least rich in lime. He watched with the greatest exactitude over the workers as they followed the indications he gave each day. He knew that the slightest error would ruin the fresco: it would not last more than three years on a poorly prepared wall.

Barbara, in the hope of hastening Mantegna's work, had sumptuous tapestries brought from Germany, depicting hunting and banqueting scenes. She refused the battle scenes that might have influenced Francesco's future for the worse, recalling that Ludovico had been nicknamed 'the Turk' in his youth.

Mantegna went to see Ludovico. Barbara was present at their meeting. 'After the usual pleasantries, not a single glance. A stony face, with pinched lips. Few words, but a rare determination: "I do not want these hangings!" said Mantegna. "They would make my painting pointless." – "They are tapestries of great value," said Ludovico, "and my wife likes them."

'In an instant, I realised that Mantegna would do nothing; he was close to abandoning any project; he was feeling discouraged. His anger concealed a sense of sadness and inexpressible despondency.

'"Let Messer Andrea do as he wishes," I said to Ludovico.

'Ludovico agreed. Mantegna took one step backwards, bowed, and left.

'Ludovico asked me why I had changed my mind so suddenly. I explained my reasons. We never referred to the matter again.

'Ever since that day, everything has changed between Mantegna and myself. He no longer judges me to be "ignorant of his art". He has said as much; I know he has: his words were reported to me.'

There is every probability that Mantegna had not only confided to Jacopo Bellini that Barbara of Brandenburg was 'ignorant of his art', but perhaps expressed himself in more colourful terms than the ones reported to Barbara. It did not bother her. She had always had the wit to make fun of herself before the others did. She pardoned Mantegna and withheld from using his insolence as a pretext for having him dismissed.

'Yesterday,' she wrote, 'I asked him if he was satisfied with my progress in the knowledge of his art. Mantegna smiled. This smile sealed our reconciliation.'

The painter often invited Barbara to come and look at the plans that he had drawn up for the different parts of the ceremonial room. Mantegna wanted to 'build an architecture that would support colour'. In order to achieve this, he mixed all the sciences, mosaics, marble, fresco painting, and used the newly discovered laws of perspective, and finally devised an oculus[6] in the form of 'a well of light falling from a pagan heaven'.

His achievement would remain unequalled.

* * *

The painted hangings constituted the axis of his composition.

Mantegna had lacemakers brought from Florence to embroider brocade designs. He observed them for hours, hesitated between several of them and eventually decided on the most complicated patterns. He copied them, and chose a red and a blue of whose vividness we can today have no idea: they were painted *a secco*, and their dazzle has been lost.

So Mantegna painted the hangings, but showed them as drawn. The curtains fall to the ground between four imitation pilasters; two others are set in the centre and two others in the corners. The hangings, instead of hiding the walls, reveal the scenes. Their presence suggests the curtain rising on the theatre that was the court of the Gonzagas in Mantua, around the years 1460. One of the curtains opens onto a loggia where Barbara and her family have gathered. The carpets covering the ground

6. A skylight in the ceiling of the Bridal Chamber.

seem to slip into the chamber itself, thus following the curve of the wall.

The Camera could only be visited at night. 'Light would ruin it,' said Mantegna. This is not true. But the master was not averse to imposing pointless constraints. They sometimes sprang from superstition, linked to the practice of his art. After all, Mantegna confessed to Jacopo Bellini that he feared he did not have the heart to finish his work, 'sensing,' he said, 'that *something* will bring me misfortune.' He was wrong. But many artists view the facility and success of their work as a bad sign. This is an inexplicable fear for those who never have to create anything. Mantegna did not escape from doubt and anguish, both before embarking on the Camera Depicta and also during its realisation.

He would often interrupt his work, complaining that 'he no longer had any strength or any desire to continue'. However, in a letter to Jacopo Bellini, he acknowledged that he had drawn encouragement from the praise of Barbara of Brandenburg.

'She consoles me,' he wrote, 'for the unprecedented difficulties I am encountering in the Camera and also for the ease of execution I sometimes experience, which is – as you will be aware – just as distressing (*sconvolgente*) as failure. Personally, I see it as a proof of negligence and mediocrity. All of the Marquise's powers of persuasion are necessary to convince me to the contrary. She succeeds very well in this, and gives me fresh courage.'

* * *

The first time that she set eyes on the Camera, Barbara was filled with enthusiasm; she was unstinting in her praise.

She wrote to Maria of Hohenzollern, 'Imagine an almost completely dark room, barely lit by candles arranged at the four corners of the room, that is illumined by gold, pink and green marble, and angels. The whole wall is sumptuously decorated. The whole thing already produced a magnificent effect when it was still on paper, but in reality it surpasses anything one can say of it.'

Mantegna designed the geometrical pattern on the plinth that runs the full length of the wall: simple oval medallions whose centres and ledges are encrusted with pink and green marble. The pilasters surmounting the plinth are decorated with gilded acanthus leaves. From the corbels placed at the top of the pilasters painted on the walls and in the corners there spring great ribs that divide the ceiling, near the oculus, into eight diamond-shaped caissons, forming semicircular lunettes along the upper part of the walls. Each lunette is adorned with an emblem painted on a shield hanging from a garland – a family emblem, such as the white dog with a collar, a leash and a muzzle, adopted around 1432 by Ludovico's father, Marquis Gian Francesco, or an emblem chosen by Ludovico himself, such as the radiant sun he adopted in 1441, after the battle of Caravaggio. The arms of the Gonzagas are depicted over the door made in the south wall. In the medallions, surrounded by a laurel crown, set into the diamond-shaped caissons, are the busts of the first eight Roman emperors, held up by *putti* who stand out against imitation gold mosaics. On the base of the vault in the triangles are depicted scenes illustrating the life of Hercules, six others the life of Orpheus, and six others that of Orion.[7]

'Ludovico feels particularly attached to Hercules; in his childhood, he was given the affectionate nickname of Hercules by Vittorino,' wrote Barbara.

In the two scenes depicted in the Camera (the announcement of Francesco's elevation and, opposite, Francesco being greeted on his entry into the town by his father and brothers), Mantegna

7. Ronald Lightbown, FMR review, no. 36.

forgot to make his characters look younger. In fact, it took almost ten years to execute the Camera, which was completed only in 1474.

Nobody complained about this forgetfulness. Barbara merely noted, 'Ludovico has eyes imbued with a weariness that I find alarming.' She did not mention the fact that, in spite of his characteristic realism, Mantegna had not painted the humps on the backs of the Gonzaga children. Only the thick mantle covering the frail shoulders of Paola, Barbara's younger daughter, barely conceals the arching of her back. Paola is offering Barbara an apple in a posture of complete submission. Her mother's gaze is directed elsewhere. Barbara never had eyes for Paola's anxious expectancy.

But Barbara did not pick up this detail, any more than she noted Mantegna's indulgence for her other children. Still, she was grateful to him for having brought out the majesty of Francesco, the cardinal.

'These paintings,' she said, 'will be more use to him than the most zealous ambassadors.'

But Francesco never became pope.

A certain bitterness and a mistrust of Rome would, as a result, linger in the Gonzaga family.

Nearly fifty years later, a desire was expressed to organise the council in Rome. Federico, Marquis of Mantua, invented numerous excuses, and pretended there were obstacles and organisational difficulties, and finally Rome decided to hold the council in Trent.

In the generations of Gonzagas that succeeded one another thereafter, none had any ambition to become pope. The contemplation of the Camera Depicta must have discouraged them from becoming involved in such a high enterprise; they contented themselves with what sufficed for their own pleasure. The truth was, they loved each other a great deal.

After seeing the oculus, Barbara of Brandenburg did not hesitate to say that Mantegna was the most marvellous painter of the day, superior to Botticelli and the Venetians.

'I have already told you,' she wrote to Maria of Hohenzollern, 'of my admiration for the court scenes, but nothing surpasses the beauty of this picture. My sole regret is that our dear Vittorino did not live long enough to see it finished.'

Vittorino da Feltre had died two years earlier. He was almost blind, and no longer writing, but Barbara insisted on keeping him with her until the end. She often spoke to him of Mantegna's Camera Depicta: Vittorino had the greatest admiration for the artist.

'I see it through your eyes,' he would say to Barbara, who reported his words to Maria of Hohenzollern.

'His dearest wish would have been to know that the Camera was finished before he died.

'I often took Vittorino to Mantegna. The smell of the pigments, the oils, the noise of sheets of paper being crumpled, the cartoons from which the outlines of the drawing were traced onto the wall – all of this enchanted him. He said that failing sight deprived him of enjoying the result of the painting, but that he was very happy to be present as it was being executed – present in a way that, doubtless, nobody had ever been before him. He could recognise Mantegna's touch – long or short, broad or narrow – from the noise of the brush.

'Mantegna told him one day that he had included his own portrait among the decorations on a pilaster.

' "I concealed myself amidst the foliage. You need a practised eye to guess at my presence."

' "So I could not dare claim to do so," said Vittorino.

' "On the contrary, my dear maestro," said Mantegna in a kindly tone.

' "And how have you depicted yourself, Messer Andrea?"

' "Looking quite furious."

' "Whatever for?" asked Vittorino.

' "For fear of looking happy, Messer Vittorino," replied Mantegna.

'Our dear Vittorino laughed uproariously at Mantegna's reply.

'I have kept this image of Vittorino da Feltre laughing and content with his lot, in spite of the harshness of his fate. This,' wrote Barbara of Brandenburg, 'consoles me for the sadness that sometimes overwhelms me without reason. Although, my dear cousin, I do not need – alas – to seek the cause for long.'

Mantegna did not want to show the ceiling of the Camera before it was completely finished. He had scaffolding erected to conceal it from everyone's sight.

'When he uncovered it, after more than a year's labours' – wrote Barbara – 'we were all overwhelmed by admiration and amazement at that joyous marvel made by Mantegna. In the skylight, under a sky in which a great cloud foams like creamy milk, young women, surrounded by angels, a Moorish woman and a peacock, are leaning over a balustrade. They seem to be filled with curiosity to see what is going on below. It took me some time to perceive the freedom with which they are dressed, so overwhelmed was I by the beauty of the spectacle. One of them is arranging her hair, only one is wearing a hat, and the Moorish woman, following the custom of her country, has her head turbaned in brightly coloured fabric. Although she is only a servant, she creates an impression of great familiarity with her mistresses. I was forgetting to mention a marvellous basket of fruit, that is miraculously held balanced on a piece of wood; it is right next to the peacock, whose plumage rivals in beauty the angels' wings.

'These angels are standing on the ledge of the balustrade. When I saw them, I was unable to hold back a cry of alarm.

' "Let me reassure Your Ladyship," said Mantegna, "the angels have wings."

' "I must confess, my eyes were deceived," I replied.

'The whole court laughed at my mistake. This good humour stayed with us.

'You never tire of looking at these angels. One is sticking his head through the balustrade, while another holds out his hand, and yet another is standing up, balancing and looking towards the interior of the balcony, turning his little buttocks to us, as pink and chubby as anyone could wish. They all exude the freshness of childhood, with a grace that my children never had. So I find myself obliged to consider them as angels, so that the sight of them will give me the greatest delight.

'Mantegna has painted them everywhere. Over the door, three angels are holding up his dedication, and two others are lying languidly at their feet. Their grace cannot be imagined or described. How can anyone communicate the tenderness of their gaze, the sweetness of their features, their dainty pink mouths that make you want to kiss them? What moves me most of all is the prettiness of their feet. You feel like taking them in your hands and holding them as if they were seashells. Their wings have the beauty of the colours of the rarest butterflies and remind us of the angels' divine nature, otherwise you would be tempted to think you are seeing marvellous children, depicted from real life, playing in all their serene beauty.

Barbara of Brandenburg always drew from the sight of this 'serene beauty' the strength not to succumb to the weight of time and misfortune, since she was far from spared. The end of her life was a series of continual sorrows.

4

The death of Ludovico Gonzaga was the first of the great misfortunes to afflict Barbara of Brandenburg.

The second was the hatred she nursed for her daughter Paola.

The third, the murder of Antonia Malatesta.

The last, the death of Maria of Hohenzollern.

* * *

After Ludovico's death, Barbara of Brandenburg forbade all access to the Camera Depicta.

When Barberina, her daughter, asked why, Barbara replied, 'Beauty is chary of emotion. It is already difficult to feel it once. Then the emotion loses its clarity and I fear we are more touched by the nostalgia of the memory beauty has left us than by the thing itself. That is why I try to take nothing for granted.'

Not even Federico had the right to go into the Camera where his father died. Barbara of Brandenburg was the only person with a key.

She now used a completely unadorned room as her chamber. At the start of her mourning period, she prayed night and day, and fasted frequently.

By her own admission, she was alarmingly thin. 'You would not recognise in this tall skinny woman, with her sallow face and her cold eyes, your cousin of bygone days,' she wrote to Maria of Hohenzollern.

Barbara shut herself away for hours, meditating on the vanity of things. She said she no longer wished to take any account of the things of this world, since she had taken too much account of them during Ludovico's life, something of which she now repented.

She confessed she felt a strong sense of displeasure at the sight of her youngest daughter Paola, without being able to understand why. Barbara of Brandenburg was eager for her to leave Mantua.

* * *

Paola was to marry the Count of Gorizia.

Paola Gonzaga was fifteen. Leonardo of Gorizia was thirty-five, but looked fifty. His domestic life had nothing in common with that of the Gonzagas. He spent his life out hunting; his court was composed of illiterate country bumpkins. Paola loved poetry and music, and was merry and charming by nature, 'the most gifted', as Vittorino said of her.

A widower, childless, heavily in debt – he had lost a portion of his lands in the Tyrol and the region of Gorizia – the Count nonetheless had some exorbitant claims to make. He expressed them straight out in a letter to Ludovico Gonzaga: 'Your daughter is a hunchback, and that requires compensation.'

Ludovico yielded on every count. His daughter's dowry amounted to ten thousand florins in gifts of every kind.

The inventory of these gifts drawn up after Paola's death fills one with amazement: jewels, clothes, fabrics, cloths and sheets, silverware, a polyptych for her chapel, an ivory chess set, four chests of great value, made by Mantegna, containing fourteen precious books including the works of Virgil, Sallust, Cicero, Dante, St Augustine and the *Triumphs* of Petrarch: a marvellous library.

'These books are the sole consolation of my life,' Paola wrote to her mother, much later.

On 11th July 1475, the contract was signed.

On 2nd September of the same year, Ludovico Gonzaga died. The date of the wedding had been set for 5th November 1475. That day remained unchanged, despite Paola's desire to postpone the union. Barbara of Brandenburg remained inflexible. 'You do not go back once you have given your word.'

On Barbara's orders, the wedding took place in a church at Bolzano, and not in Mantua. The Bishop of Trent and Ludovico the Younger (Paola's brother) officiated.

Not a note of music was played to celebrate this union, no feast was laid on, there was not the slightest sign of joy at court or in town, but the silence that follows desolation. Mantua was in mourning for its prince.

Straight after the ceremony, Paola removed her bridal veil and replaced it by a heavy black veil covering her face.

That very same evening, when the Count of Gorizia came for the woman who had become his wife, he tore off her veil and forbade her ever to wear it again. In spite of Paola's pleadings ('I knelt before him, my face wet with tears'), the Count of Gorizia did not give way. It seems that he had hated Paola from the minute he set eyes on her.

The wedding night was dreadful. Ignorant of the things of love, and imagining them after the fashion of courtly love that she had encountered in books and Vittorino's lessons, she did not expect Gorizia to be so brutal. Half drunk, he took her 'like a beast' (*una bestia*), as she wrote to her mother. We know the reply Barbara wrote in consolation.

The next day, Paola was found by her *cameriera*, half unconscious. She was so seriously ill that fears were expressed for her life.

The procession of the newly-wed that would travel from Mantua to Innsbruck was able to set off only four weeks later, at dawn, in the freezing cold.

Ludovico, who was filled with compassion for his sister, wanted to accompany her to her new residence. Although her suite was composed of thirty people, Paola greeted this news with joy.

However much Barbara told Ludovico how pointless it was, he would not give up his plan, harbouring as he did the most intense worries about Paola.

Ludovico kept Barbara informed at every stage of his journey. 'It never ends,' he wrote to her mother. 'Paola is exhausted. She has great dark shadows under her eyes. My poor sister hardly touches her food, she is not sleeping well, she never gets any real rest. Luisa, her lady-in-waiting, and I do not leave her a single instant. Her husband does not seem in the slightest worried by her state. He is only interested in the next stop, in what he is going to eat and drink and especially whether he will be able to go hunting for a few hours, to stretch his legs and blow away the cobwebs, as he says. Our presence is hateful to him and he does not hide the fact.'

Finally, after three weeks' journey, they arrived at the castle of Bruck, in Lienz.

'Our arrival in that dreary land,' wrote Ludovico, 'in that unfurnished palace with its arid and desolate surroundings, was the most melancholy thing it has ever been my privilege to see.'

Barbara replied, 'Those desolate landscapes, that dreary town! So does nothing meet with favour in your eyes in that country which is mine and thus also, to some extent, yours?'

Everything that would have offended her elsewhere, here found its *raison d'être*. Barbara of Brandenburg had become malicious.

When Paola set eyes on this gloomy palace, she fainted away in her brother's arms. Ludovico decided to stay on until she was completely recovered. He had no confidence in the Count.

Barbara ordered Ludovico to return at the earliest possible opportunity: 'Your presence can only aggravate a sorrow that Paola is determined to indulge in however she can, and you are not in the least sure of her.'

Ludovico left the castle of Bruck three weeks later. Paola's farewell to her brother was harrowing, and Ludovico left feeling broken-hearted.

Paola continually begged her mother to let her come to Mantua for a while, whereupon Barbara wrote to the Count of Gorizia, whom she called 'her dear son-in-law', not to yield to her daughter's whims.

Ludovico intervened and Barbara assured Paola that it was her dearest wish to welcome her to Mantua.

At the same time, she took measures to find a pretext that would delay her arrival, fixed another date not too long after the first, and again postponed *sine die* the break she had promised her daughter.

Barbara endlessly repeated things she had already heard.

'This,' wrote Paola, 'has sowed confusion in the Count's mind. He does not understand these complications. He views them as a trick I am playing on him and refuses to grant me any more concessions. He will not allow me to go to Mantua, suspecting as he does some plot on the part of our family. These days, his behaviour towards me has been that of a real enemy.'

It would be several months before Paola dared again to ask her husband for permission to travel. Realising that he was fighting a losing battle, he gave in.

The date for Paola's stay in Mantua was settled. She was just about to leave when an emissary from the Mantuan court presented himself. Barbara was ill; in these circumstances, she forbade her daughter from undertaking 'such a long journey'.

'Ludovico,' she wrote, 'is at my side, and he will confirm that it is impossible to receive you just now.'

At the foot of the page, a few words from Ludovico to Paola did indeed confirm his mother's message.

Paola then wrote to her brother, 'I refuse to live nursing a hope that has foundered on a refusal I cannot understand. My disappointment is so great, and I am going through such terrible times as a result, that I prefer to live in the idea that I will never again see Mantua, nor you, my dear brother. Indeed, God is my witness that this is my dearest hope, but I do not know of any worse sorrow than this joy that I have nursed for months on end, this journey which has been planned and organised down to the smallest details, and which I have suddenly been forced to abandon.

'I can no longer stand seeing this joy snatched from me at the last minute. This cruelty is exhausting my strength, which is already limited; it is barely enough to keep me alive. I no longer have the courage to struggle. The Count himself has taken pity on me. He has suggested that I go and take the waters, but I have abandoned that idea too. I no longer take pleasure in anything.'

Ludovico invited Paola to pray, so that she could forget the world's wickedness.

Paola replied, 'The wickedness of the world is not enough; it is the world itself which I must try to forget.'

After two years of marriage, Paola gave birth to a daughter. The child, named Barbara, was baptised on the same night she was born, because of the weakness of her constitution. She died three days afterwards. Paola would never get over it. The letters she sent imploring them to let her return to Mantua (*vi supplico*) were gradually followed by silence. Until her death, which occurred almost fifteen years after Barbara's, she would ask the Gonzagas for nothing more.

Paola died without having seen Barbara again, nor Ludovico, her beloved brother; nor Mantua, Mantegna's Camera, or the Gonzaga chapel, which Paola claimed to prize above all else.

Barbara never felt any remorse at having failed in compassion towards her daughter. In the course of one conversation, Ludovico rebuked her for this.

While he was in Verona, Barbara of Brandenburg returned to the comments she had made about Paola before Ludovico's departure.

She wrote, 'I aspire to nothing other than tranquillity of soul, which will let nothing disturb it.'

5

'I recognise in Federico nothing of Ludovico's wisdom,' wrote Barbara of Brandenburg to Maria of Hohenzollern. 'I find in him nothing but a strange madness which he tries to tame – in vain, for his struggle is unavailing.

'Federico's only loves are hunting and music, the only times when he can find a little serenity. He cannot get off to sleep without listening to music. He sometimes summons his musicians in the middle of the night. He can be found wandering round the castle looking for them. Several musicians have fled Mantua, exhausted by so many constraints. Which artist could resist such a barbarous way of practising his art?'

Barbara of Brandenburg kept aloof from power. Francesco, the son she preferred best of all, lived in Rome. Ludovico the Younger had no liking for anything but pleasure and gambling, and lived regretting the fact that he had not been able to save – as he wrote to Francesco – his sister Paola 'from the clutches of the Count of Gorizia'.

'He is trying to take his mind off things,' wrote Barbara to Maria of Hohenzollern.

Barberina was the only one who lived as she really wished. 'She is surrounded by artists. I am keeping up a sustained correspondence with several of them. I have had certain codices sent to Barberina – they have aroused the admiration of the court of Württemberg.'

However, Barberina wrote to her mother, 'The German climate suits me better than does ours. I have never felt better than when I was far from Lombardy and its leaden sky.'

'The sky of Lombardy is leaden only for you,' replied Barbara. 'For those who look at it properly, it is clear and light, but I am not fooled when you talk about another kind of sky than ours, and I hope with all my heart that the sky of Württemberg will never see its light clouded.'

At the end of 1479, Barbara complained of the monotony of her life. 'My inspiration has dried up: old age holds my imagination in its grip like a gangue,' she wrote to Maria.

Barbara continued to recite lines from Petrarch or Dante, but her pleasure was ruined. 'There is no one around me to hear them: all my friends are dead.'

At Christmas 1479, a drama came to break the monotony of Barbara of Brandenburg's life. She recounted the events to Maria of Hohenzollern:

How foolish I was to complain of the tedium of my life! I could hardly have hoped for anything better designed to bring it so overwhelmingly to nought. I have lost all peace of mind. The horrific vision of that blood on the snow continually pursues me.

On that day, cursed above all others, it was freezing hard. In the middle of the day, the sky was so black that darkness had already fallen. It had been snowing for three days. Nobody was surprised when Rodolfo decided he would like to go out for a ride into the countryside. Everyone knows that since childhood he has liked to sniff the tang of the snow and head off on a steaming horse with a foam-flecked bit, galloping along until he has exhausted himself.

So Rodolfo put on a leather jerkin, threw over his shoulders a thick fox-fur greatcoat, pulled on leather boots laced to the knees and put on a fur bonnet with a helmet over it, which gave him a strange appearance; those who saw him did not fail to remark on it. It was Giulio Moser, his closest friend, who told him he had read in the stars that he must always protect his head to preserve his life. Given the intense cold, it was not difficult for Rodolfo to obey.

Thus attired, he chose the swiftest steed and, apart from one man to whom he spoke, who knew everything and yet would do nothing to prevent the irreparable, nobody had any idea of what was going to happen.

After galloping for over three hours, my son arrived in Luzzara. The whole castle was asleep. Rodolfo awoke his young wife, the lovely Antonia Malatesta, dragged her by force into the snow-covered gardens, ran her through with a sword, and returned to Mantua to seek the protection of his brother Federico, who granted it to him.

In the morning, Antonia was found dead, her face battered, her body frozen, like a rose in the snow.

When he saw his brother unkempt, his face clawed, panting and foaming at the lips and trembling with rage, Federico did not have the courage – as his father would assuredly have done – to exile him, and immediately granted him his clemency, for fear that he too might end up with a sword through him.

As a final precaution, Federico banished for ever from Mantua Rodolfo's friend who had accused Antonia of adultery, and thus caused all the guilt to fall on his own head.

The horror of the crime is always present before my eyes, and every time I see my son, I shudder with disgust.

Rodolfo sensed the disgust he inspired in all. He did not stay in Mantua for long. He signed up in the Imperial army. 'He seeks death on every battlefield in Europe,' wrote Barbara, 'but he always comes away safe and sound. Will this slowness in dying, which he owes to his valour alone, redeem the great flaws in his heart? God will reveal the answer to him soon enough,' concluded Barbara of Brandenburg.

Rodolfo found death at the Battle of Taro, in 1495. He too perished by the sword, his forehead split open, as had been foretold to him.

* * *

Shortly after this crime, Barbara learnt that Maria of Hohenzollern was seriously ill and was asking for her. Barbara of Brandenburg refused to see her. Maria would never forgive her. Against all expectation, she had a few months' remission. She no longer replied to her cousin's letters. All correspondence between them was broken off.

Then Barbara seemed to succumb to depression, and no longer took pleasure in anything. She often asked Ludovico to stay with her and tell her the names of things. 'Words,' she told him, 'slip across my memory like water, following their own whim. When I think I am about to grasp them, they escape me like capricious little imps.'

She never asked for her other children. 'My presence,' wrote Ludovico, 'seems to appease a little the terror that can always be read in her face.'

Barbara emerged from her silence less and less frequently. Ludovico rarely visited her, occupied as he was by his pleasures. A *cameriera* kept watch over Barbara night and day. They feared she might run away from the Castello di San Giorgio, as she had once already. One night, barefoot, she tried to get back to Brandenburg to see the castle of Johann the Alchemist, her father.

'Federico scolded her severely,' wrote Ludovico.

He asked Paola to come and visit her mother. Paola refused.

The melancholy of Barbara of Brandenburg alarmed Federico. He would visit her only in the company of a large number of courtiers.

'Even in his presence, our mother will sometimes talk to herself. Federico cannot stand this. I pointed out to him that our mother's words were all sensible and considered, which greatly consoled him, not for her sake, as you can imagine, my dear brother, but for his own,' wrote Ludovico to Francesco.

* * *

In April 1480, Maria of Hohenzollern died.

'The death of her cousin, whom she had cherished since childhood,' wrote Ludovico to Francesco, 'has left our mother in the greatest distress. However, one of the strange reasons that aggravates her despair is the fact that her grief is not as great as she had imagined.

' "My heart is dry," she told me, "that's a bad sign."

'Otherwise, she barely speaks. Her *cameriera* says that she is sweet-tempered and obedient, and the great outbursts of anger that used to shake her have died away. She sometimes utters our father's name in a low voice, and if the *cameriera* points this out to her, she shudders like someone who has just been awoken with a start. I told the *cameriera* to leave her alone with her dreams, and not to be brusque with her in any way, but to satisfy her every wish, if possible.'

6

At the approach of her death, Barbara of Brandenburg had herself carried into the Camera Depicta. She had the ceremonial bed placed under Mantegna's oculus.

When she entered her death agony, Barbara lost the use of her voice. In the hours leading up to her death, she did utter a few phrases that nobody could grasp: Barbara was speaking the language of her childhood, which nobody there spoke.

The last thing she saw before dying was the face of the women leaning over her, the smiling Moorish woman and, in the cerulean sky painted by Mantegna, angels at play.

It seemed to Ludovico, who recorded this scene, that Barbara was half-smiling. He told Federico as much. The latter came over to the bed, and murmured a few words in his mother's ear. She did not reply. Then Federico placed a mirror in front of her mouth. It did not mist over. Barbara of Brandenburg was dead.

Ludovico touched her eyelids gently with his fingertips, and swiftly closed her eyes.

Afterword

There never was any correspondence between Barbara of Brandenburg and Maria of Hohenzollern (who never existed); nor between Mantegna and his father-in-law Jacopo Bellini, or Vittorino da Feltre and Carlo or Ludovico Gonzaga, and certainly not Gregorio Simeone, who never saw the light of day.

The marquis of Ventivoglio never possessed a collection that was dispersed at his death, since he himself was a fictitious character, and Montaigne never went to Mantua.

I hope that the curator of the print room in Mantua (if there is one) will not be cross with me for having given him an imaginary identity and having quoted, as if it were by him, an imaginary work (*Lettere di Barbara di Brandeburgo*).

I imagine that Mantegna never drew on the services of lacemakers, but he did paint the Camera Depicta, just as it can still be seen today in the Palazzo di San Giorgio.

Barbara of Brandenburg did exist. What was her life like? I do not know. I have gathered a few scattered details, found in an article by Maria Bellonci[8] on the Gonzagas; I have already mentioned how much I am indebted to Ronald Lightbown.

All of this is a game, a kind of 'novel' whose characters I have depicted in the milieu of fifteenth-century Italy.

8. 'Portrait de famille', FMR review, no. 36.